Connect is published by Stone Arch Books
A Capstone Imprint
1710 Roe Crest Drive
North Mankato, Minnesota 56003
www.capstonepub.com

Library of Congress Cataloging-in-Publication Data
Gunderson, Jessica, author.
 The songs of Stones River : a Civil War novel / by Jessica Gunderson; cover illustration by Anthony J. Foti.
     pages cm. — (The Civil War)
 Summary: In late 1862 young James of Murfreesboro is a proud Southerner who takes on the responsibility of providing for his newly widowed mother and younger sister by working for his neighbor alongside the field slave Eli — an experience that calls into question many of his cherished beliefs about slavery and the War.
 ISBN 978-1-4342-9703-7 (library binding) — ISBN 978-1-4342-9704-4 (pbk.)
1. Slaves—Tennessee—Juvenile fiction. 2. African Americans—Tennessee—Juvenile fiction. 3. Teenage boys—Tennessee—Juvenile fiction. 4. Stones River, Battle of, Murfreesboro, Tenn., 1862-1863—Juvenile fiction. 5. Murfreesboro (Tenn.)—History—Juvenile fiction. 6. Tennessee—History—Civil War, 1861–1865—Juvenile fiction. 7. United States—History—C ivil War, 1861–1865—Juvenile fiction. [1. Slavery—Fiction. 2. African Americans—Fiction. 3. Stones River, Battle of, Murfreesboro, Tenn., 1862–1863--Fiction. 4. Murfreesboro (Tenn.)—History—Civil War, 1861–1865—Fiction. 5. Tennessee—History—Civil War, 1861–1865—Fiction. 6. United States—History—Civil War, 1861–1865—Fiction.] I. Foti, Anthony J., illustrator. II. Title.
 PZ7.G963So 2015
 813.6—dc23   2014025995

Designer:
Veronica Scott

Cover illustration:
Tony Foti

Printed in China.
092014 008472RRDS15

THE SONGS OF
STONES RIVER

A CIVIL WAR NOVEL

BY JESSICA GUNDERSON

CHAPTER 1

YANKEE BETRAYAL

OCTOBER, 1862
MURFREESBORO, TENNESSEE

James

"Get on your Yankee horse and ride on outta here!"

Those were the last words I said to my best friend, Stefan, after he told me he was joining up. I wouldn't have minded if he'd joined the Confederates. In fact, I might've followed him.

But no. He was joining up with the bloody Yanks.

We'd been walking along Stones River, near our town of Murfreesboro, Tennessee. As usual, we were headed toward our favorite spot to catch catfish. The river flowed as peacefully as ever, and birds whistled and swooped above us. The war seemed to have no effect on nature. Those birds chirped away happily, not knowing that in nearby battlefields, men were falling dead and bloodying the soil.

I could tell there was something on Stefan's mind.

He was always quiet and thoughtful, but today his silence was punctuated by a worried line across his brow.

"You think this war will ever come to an end?" Stefan said at last. He didn't look at me as he spoke, just stabbed at the earth with a long stick.

"Yep," I answered. "Our boys will fight until the South is finally free."

Stefan fell silent again. We never talked much about the war, partly because we were only twelve years old and would rather run around the woods than talk, but mostly because we just didn't agree. Stefan and his family were Unionists, which meant they were against the war. They wanted the South to stay in the Union. I, on the other hand, firmly believed in the Southern cause. The Confederates could build a great country. We didn't need the North telling us what to do.

"My great-grandfather gave his life to win independence from the British," Stefan said.

"And my *father* gave his life to win independence from the North!" I retorted. I grabbed the stick from Stefan's hand and threw it into the river. Tears churned just behind my eyeballs. The pain of losing my father was still deep and raw. I wouldn't let Stefan see me cry.

"Our country is worth fightin' for," Stefan went on.

"Sure is," I muttered.

"James, I'm joining up," Stefan said. His words tumbled out, tripping over each other. "I'm gonna go to Kentucky. Maybe join the Ohio infantry. Maybe be a drummer boy or help at the field hospitals. I know I ain't old enough to fight, but I *look* old and can shoot a pigeon from a fencepost from near a mile. I can't sit by no more and watch —"

"Hold on," I said. My heart was hammering and my blood boiled, though my skin felt frozen as ice. "You're joinin' the *Yanks*?"

"I'm sorry, James. I know your daddy —"

"Don't you be bringin' up my daddy!" I shouted. "You're about to buddy up with the very scoundrels who killed him!"

"I gotta do what's right. I gotta preserve the Union."

"No. What you gotta do is get out of my face!" I hollered. I doubled my fists, ready to take a swing at him. But he just stood there, looking solemn. And those blasted birds were still twittering away.

In the end, I didn't swing at him. I spat in the dirt then whirled away and ran as fast as my legs could carry me. "Get on your Yankee horse and ride on outta here!" I yelled over my shoulder.

"James, wait!" Stefan called.

But I didn't turn around, just kept running as though the Yanks themselves were after me.

∽

Back before the war, we didn't pay much attention to the political talk of our fathers. We didn't understand it much. All we knew was that my father wanted Tennessee to secede from the Union, and Stefan's father didn't. When Tennessee finally did secede, I felt a little victorious, as though my family was right and his wasn't. But I didn't lord it over him.

After the war broke out in 1861, we never thought the fighting would reach Tennessee. South Carolina, where the war had started, was far off. Word leaked in about battles in Virginia. Most were Confederate victories, like the Battle of Bull Run. I thought we'd lick them Yanks quick, and the Confederacy would be free.

At first, Stefan and I thought war was glorious. We fought pretend battles along the banks of the river. Sometimes we were on the same side, dodging an unseen enemy that lurked in the trees. Other times we pretended he was a Yank and I was a Rebel, and we'd shoot at each other with our finger and thumb.

I never thought our little games would turn into a grim reality.

The months dragged on, and no side showed signs of giving up. Winter fell, and the war came closer. Both sides wanted control of our humble state of Tennessee, mostly due to the railroads that crisscrossed the state. Yankee victories at Fort Donelson and Shiloh nearly tore our hearts out.

Then the Yankees took over our state capital, Nashville, just thirty miles away.

Soon, Yankee soldiers flooded Murfreesboro, using our railroad to supply their troops. They came into our homes and took our weapons. Any man who didn't sign an oath of allegiance to the United States was thrown in jail.

My father refused to sign.

That's when my father left his job at the bank and joined the Confederate Army under General Forrest. My life would never be the same again.

As I walked toward home, my belly burned with anger. How could Stefan join up with the very scoundrels who'd killed my father?

CHAPTER 2

MAN OF THE HOUSE

James

I'd never forget the day my father died, nearly three months ago, though it felt like ages.

It was July 12, 1862, and hotter than blazes. Union General Thomas Crittenden had set up forts around town, and we Southerners hunkered in our houses, not wanting to even pass the Yanks on the street.

But General Forrest and our soldiers were about to surprise ol' Crittenden. Just before dawn, I woke to the roar of gunshots. I crept to the window and saw a magnificent sight.

Our gray-coated soldiers thundered past, whooping and hollering as they stormed into the town square to release prisoners from the courthouse. It was too dark to see faces, but I knew my daddy was among them.

The Yankees stumbled about in confusion, some half-dressed and still half-asleep.

The sun rose high and bright. All morning, bullets cracked and bayonets clanged. We were whipping the Yanks good, driving them out of our town and back to the North where they belonged.

That afternoon, Crittenden and his miserable souls surrendered. With the fighting over, I ran to the street to rejoice.

But when I opened the front door, I saw my dad's friend Mr. Pitt and a gray-coated officer on our porch, looking forlorn. They didn't have to say a word. I knew right then my daddy was dead. I was only twelve, but I was the man of the house.

My daddy was dead, and my mother, my little sister, and I were barely getting by.

My sister and I didn't even go to school anymore because our schoolhouse had been turned into a hospital. My plump, rosy-cheeked Mama had turned into a skinny, old woman. My sister whined nonstop about being hungry. I spent my days fishing and hunting, trying to feed them and put some color back in their cheeks.

Now I was returning home with no fish — and all

because my traitorous friend was joining up with the Yanks.

My thoughts did nothing but stir up anger inside me. I stomped toward home, where my mama was at her usual spot on the front porch swing. She never swung anymore, just sat still, looking far off at nothing.

She turned her head slightly as I approached. "James?" she said.

"Hello, Mama. Did you eat today?" I asked.

She tried to smile, but her lips only turned downward. "Yes," she said. But I knew she hadn't.

"Where's Nellie?" I asked, looking around for my nine-year-old sister.

Mama blinked at me, then shrugged and looked away.

I opened the door and a waft of burnt air hit my nostrils. I went into the kitchen and saw Nellie poking at what looked like a pan of black, misshapen rocks. Turrets of smoke rose from the pan.

Nellie turned to me. One of the crispy lumps quivered in her outstretched palm. "Would you like a biscuit?" she asked, her blue eyes watery with tears.

I wanted nothing to do with the blackened lump, but I smiled and said, "Sure!"

As I bit into the scorched biscuit, I tried not to

worry. I knew Nellie had used the last of our flour to make the burned biscuits. And Daddy's war pension still hadn't come. Where would we find the money to buy more?

CHAPTER 3

SEASON OF CHANGE

Eli

I don't reckon why anyone would want to hear my story. I weren't nothin' but a slave boy. I ain't never been nothin' special.

When the war came, I heard talk at the general store that it were all about us slaves. But I didn't believe it. I couldn't read, but I could listen. I listened good. And I reckoned the war were less about us and more about money. Them Northerners didn't want to lose the South and all the money we brought 'em from farmin' cotton.

My life weren't too hard, truth be told. At least, not afore Missus Pitt died. She were kind enough, kept Massah Pitt from beatin' me and my mama too bad.

But then, two years ago now, times got tough. Massah lost some money somehow, and a bunch of his land. Two field slaves run off. Massah hired a hunting party, but they never caught 'em. It were just me to tend the farm and fields. I s'pose he couldn't afford to buy any new slaves.

One night I heard Missus and Massah talkin' in the foyer. Missus Pitt was sayin' she was strong and able. Didn't need my mama no more. She could carry the housework herself.

So soon after, they sold my mama. She went for a good price, I hear. Made me a bit proud, to be honest. Even though I felt like my whole heart was sold along with her.

What I missed most about my mama was her music. She sang all the day and night. Even when she was only talkin', her words sounded like a song.

If I listened hard, I could hear her songs in the chirps of birds and the whistle of the wind. And that helped me some. I felt she was near, even though she was far off.

Missus Pitt did a good job on the housework. I reckon she learnt a lot from watching my mama. But then she got sick and died, and Massah had to buy a new slave girl. Turned out sellin' my mama was all for nothing.

Everything got bad for me after that. Seemed like I couldn't do nothin' right, even though I worked harder'n ever. Hardly slept a wink. When the war broke out, Massah got anger in his eyes every time he looked at me. Like he blamed me.

Last spring, the worst happened. Our milk cow Betsy was about to give birth, and Massah had a man lined up to buy the calf. I spent nights in the barn, at the ready for when her time came. I weren't too worried. I'd been birthin' calves since the day I was born.

I must've fell asleep. I dreamt my mama was callin' for me. I jerked awake and saw that it weren't my mama callin'. It was Betsy the cow. She made the most awful sounds. Something was wrong.

I had no time to call for Massah. I ran over and helped Betsy bring out the calf best I could. But that calf was deader than a doornail.

I guess it were my fault for falling asleep. I deserved the beating I got that day. But the beatings didn't stop with just the one. From then on, I woke to beatings and went to bed with beatings. I couldn't hardly sleep from being so sore.

I figured Massah would get rid of me. But I guess no one wanted me.

A few months later the Union soldiers came, then the Confederates, and the war was at our doorstep. A friend of Massah Pitt's got killed in the fighting. After that, he seemed to forget about beating me, so I guess the war was good for that.

Then it was fall, and the leaves were turning bright colors before falling to the ground. I was feeling good as I trudged out to the barn to milk Betsy. Fall always seemed to me the season of change.

I swung open the barn door. That's when I knew change had happened, and it weren't good. Betsy was dead.

CHAPTER 4

OPPORTUNITY

James

I couldn't sleep. My thoughts jumped from Stefan to the hunger in my stomach. We had no one to turn to, no other family to speak of. I had cousins in eastern Tennessee, a slew of boys and one girl, but we barely knew them. We hadn't seen them since their mama, my mama's sister, died years ago. Mama didn't care much for her sister's husband — a boisterous, brash man who was never silent in his opinions. And she didn't approve of how he let the kids run wild, even the girl.

We couldn't turn to them for help. We had no one.

The next morning Mama seemed in better spirits. I hoped it meant she was finally getting over Daddy's death. I dared not tell her Stefan had joined the Yanks. She'd always had a spot in her heart for Stefan and baked him special cakes whenever he came to our house.

Mama boiled a pot of coffee on the stove and handed Nellie and me a mug apiece. "It's fixin' to be a chilly day, by the looks of it," Mama said. "This'll warm your insides."

She smiled at us, and I smiled back. A quick glance told me Nellie wasn't smiling at all. Her mouth was set in a firm line.

Mama didn't seem to notice. "Shall we head to the church this afternoon?" she asked Nellie. "The ladies are knitting socks to send to our soldiers."

"I don't want any part of this war," Nellie spat.

Mama's smile broke. "But Nellie," she said, "the cold is settin' in. Without warm socks, our boys' feet will freeze right off! And without feet, our boys can't march. And if they can't march, we can't win the war!" Mama attempted a smile again, but Nellie's face didn't change.

"I'm hungry," Nellie said finally.

"Let me just stir you up some cakes and bacon," Mama said, heading toward the pantry.

I wanted to keep her from seeing we had no flour. I stepped in front of her with a forced grin. "Mama, why don't you sit down and rest?" I said. "I'll tend to Nellie."

Mama brushed me aside and opened the pantry door. "Oh mercy, where is the flour?"

"I used it all while you were settin' on your porch swing!" Nellie yelled. "Now there ain't none."

Mama's face turned ghostly white. "None?" she whispered. Her body swayed, and I caught her before she fell to the floor.

"Oh, James, what will we do?" she murmured into my shoulder.

"Don't you worry, Mama. I was just fixin' to buy us food anyhow. I got some money," I said, knowing it was a lie.

But my words didn't seem to soothe her. Her shoulders trembled as I led her to the front room, where she collapsed onto the sofa.

"Be strong, Mama," I told her, shooting Nellie an angry look before heading out the door.

I was cheered a bit by news on the square. *The Daily Rebel Banner* announced a victory at Hatchie's Bridge. Even as I felt a spring in my step, I remembered Stefan. Every victory from now on would mean his defeat. Maybe even his death.

I sat down on the steps of the courthouse, my back against one of the wide, white pillars. This very spot had been a battle site just a few months ago. I imagined my father charging valiantly up the steps, musket in hand, ready to release the prisoners. I imagined him picking off a dozen Yankees before falling to the ground. He was a hero, dying for the cause he believed in.

I wished I could fight, too. Sure I was young, but boys younger than me were out there on the battlefields. But I couldn't. I had to stay put and take care of my mama and my sister.

As I sat pondering, I saw Mr. Pitt, Daddy's friend, moving hurriedly across the square. He looked in a foul mood, though he tossed me a rough smile and tipped his hat. I stood up as he approached.

"Good day, James. How is your mother?"

"She's faring quite well," I told him. My second lie of the day.

Mr. Pitt seemed to see right through my lie. "Nobody's faring well these days, James. I have a mind to give it all up, myself."

"Give up what, sir?"

"The farm. This life. Head out west to Texas, maybe. There ain't much here for me these days. Mrs. Pitt and I, we never had any children. And if we had, they'd be starving anyhow."

My stomach growled loudly in response, and I nodded.

"My slave boy ain't worth much," Mr. Pitt went on.

"Takes him two weeks to do a half-day's work. I got a bit of money to buy another, but these days no one's selling."

At his words an idea hit me. I saw a way to get us by, and I spoke quickly, trying to hide the desperation in my voice.

"Mr. Pitt," I said. "I'd be willin' to come help you out. I don't know much about farming, but I know a little. And I learn fast. The schoolteacher always gave me high marks. I'll work harder than any slave boy you could purchase. And I'll work for just five dollars a day."

Mr. Pitt regarded me. Jagged lines furrowed his brow. "Well now, James. You know I held your father in high esteem. But —"

"Sir, I don't mean disrespect. But that farm's been in Mrs. Pitt's family for generations. To let it go would dishonor her memory."

Mr. Pitt still seemed doubtful, so I decided to give him my final plea, much as it hurt my pride. "Mr. Pitt, I'll tell you the truth. We have no money to speak of. Daddy's pension hasn't come, and it might never. And my mama ain't doing too well. To worry her with money would send her deep into the well of despair."

Mr. Pitt nodded and held out his hand. "Seems like

a solution for the time being, James. Come on out to the farm at daybreak, and I'll show you what needs to be done afore winter."

I grasped his hand and shook it firmly, like a man would. "I look forward to it, sir."

He turned to walk away, then paused and turned back. "One more thing. I'll pay you two dollars a day for good work. For bad work, you'll get nothing. Understood?"

I nodded. It wasn't much, especially since a Confederate dollar was worth less every day. But two dollars would have to do.

CHAPTER 5

JUST A SLAVE

Eli

I got a sore beating after Betsy the cow died. Then Massah Pitt rode off toward town. While he were gone I worked best I could, even though my back was bloody from Massah Pitt's switch. I threw corn at the chickens and watched them scurry and bump for the food. One of them chickens would make for our meal tonight, if Massah Pitt was kind enough to let me eat. Those chickens were so simple-minded they didn't know one of 'em was gonna die.

Sometimes I wished to be as simple as them.

A cold wind was whipping up. Winter'd be here soon enough. We had lots of work round the farm before the cold hit. The roof on the barn needed to be patched, fields cleared, firewood chopped, meat salted and put in the cellar. I knew what needed doing, but Massah Pitt didn't trust me no more.

I couldn't help but think about them two slaves who

run off, Rufus and Jed. I remembered the fury that dropped on me. They left me, just a boy, to handle the farm myself. And not once did they ask me to escape with 'em. I wouldn't have left my mama anyhow. But now my mama was gone anyway, so it didn't matter.

I wondered where Rufus and Jed were now. If freedom suited them. I weren't sure it would suit me. I was just a slave like my mama, and like her mama before her, and her mama before her. We didn't know nothin' else.

CHAPTER 6

WATER

James

I set out toward Mr. Pitt's farm before dawn. My stomach rumbled. I'd left before Mama and Nellie were awake, and my scrounging in the pantry left me empty-handed and empty-stomached.

As I rode, the blue night changed to gray dawn, and soon pink streaks appeared above the dark Tennessee hills. I quickened my horse. Morning was coming fast. I'd best not be late on my first day.

Mr. Pitt's farm was small for the area. He'd once grown large fields of tobacco, but he lost most of his fields before the war due to his love of gambling. He'd bet his fields in late-night poker games with his neighbors, and he'd lost. Now he had just a smattering of corn fields and small tobacco crops.

My father had once said he'd never seen a man fall so fast and so hard. I resolved, in the memory of my father, to help bring Mr. Pitt's farm into good standing.

Mr. Pitt was standing on his porch, in the red glare of sunrise, with his shotgun cradled against his shoulder.

I galloped up the drive. "Sir," I called breathlessly. "I'm sorry I'm late —"

He scowled at me and barked, "I expect timeliness, James. The morning hours are crucial. You've now lost a good hour of work. So today, you'll only receive half a day's pay. Do you understand?"

I wanted to explain that I hadn't timed my journey right. I hadn't known how long it would take to get to the farm. But I only nodded silently.

Mr. Pitt still looked angry. "Not much of your father's son, are you?"

His words burned into me. I felt my cheeks redden with anger and shame. But he was right. My father would never have been late.

"Take this gun," he said, holding out his shotgun. "It's loaded. Keep it close to you at all times." He lowered his voice. "Everywhere, slaves are running off and heading north. If you see one, don't hesitate to shoot."

"Yessir," I said, taking the gun. But in my heart, I doubted I could ever shoot anyone, even a slave. I hoped I wouldn't ever be faced with the choice.

"First thing we need to do is ready the barn for winter. The roof needs a bit of patching up, but otherwise it's in good shape," Mr. Pitt told me.

We rounded the corner of the house. The barn sure didn't look like it was in good shape. It was an old, rickety structure that looked as though even a small breeze might topple it. Looking at the barn's slant, I thought it would be best to tear it down and build a new one, but I dared not say a word.

"I got a slave boy named Eli," Mr. Pitt said. "Like I told you, he ain't worth much. He's as lazy as they come. You keep after him and make sure he does what he's told. You hear?"

"Yessir," I promised.

Mr. Pitt shoved open the barn door and hollered, "Boy!"

At his call, the slave boy jumped from the hayloft and hurried toward us. He looked to be about my age, but he was taller and wider in the shoulders. I stood as tall as I could and looked him over. Firm, thick muscles lined his arms. He sure didn't look like he'd been lazy a day in his life.

As Mr. Pitt told him what we were to do, Eli kept his eyes to the ground and murmured, "Yessir."

After Mr. Pitt strode out of the barn, I followed Eli

up the ladder into the hayloft, where we'd begin patching the inside of the roof. He pointed out the spots where the leaks were the worst, and we set to patching.

I'd never imagined myself working alongside a slave, doing the work a slave does. I felt a sense of shame.

We didn't say a word to each other through the morning. The hard work caused sweat to bubble and run down my forehead. But Eli didn't seem one bit tired. I even thought I heard him humming a tune, but when I glanced over, he stopped.

Around noon, I wiped my brow and sighed. "I need rest and a bit of water," I said to Eli.

He nodded.

I headed toward the ladder but paused when Eli didn't follow me. "Are you coming?" I asked.

"No, sir. I don't rest until Massah Pitt tells me to."

I'd never had anyone call me sir before. But I can't say it made me feel proud. Instead, I felt embarrassed and uncomfortable.

I wondered if I should wait, too, but my throat was parched and thick. I slipped down the ladder and went out into the yard, looking around for Mr. Pitt. I thought he'd be out tending the fields or working in the yard, but he was nowhere to be seen.

I walked to the well and gulped down a ladle of cold, clear water. It seemed the best water I'd ever tasted.

As I leaned against the well and let the October breeze cool my forehead, I thought about Eli still working in the hot hayloft. I'd never spent much time around slaves before. My father hadn't been a slaveholder. Some rich families in Murfreesboro had house slaves, but most of us common folk did our own work. Sometimes while riding through the countryside, I'd seen slaves working in tobacco and cotton fields. I never thought much about it. It was just a way of life. And that's what this war was all about, preserving our way of life.

After the war started, I once asked my father if slavery was right or wrong.

"It doesn't matter," he'd answered. "We should be able to decide for ourselves. The federal government shouldn't decide for us."

I couldn't argue with his logic, and we never discussed slavery again.

I drank down another ladle of water. Then I made a decision without thinking twice about the consequences. I filled the ladle and walked slowly to the barn so as not to spill.

Eli had climbed down from the loft and was cleaning out a stall. The neck of his shirt had slipped down, and in the light of the open barn door, I saw jagged, white scars across his shoulders.

I averted my eyes. "Drink this," I said.

Eli turned and wiped his brow. He eyed the ladle I held out to him. "No, sir," he said.

I hadn't expected him to say no. "Mr. Pitt put me in charge," I said. "And I'm ordering you to drink it."

Eli dropped the pitchfork. His eyes burned with anger. He grabbed the ladle and took a sip.

Just then, a shadow darkened the door. I turned to see Mr. Pitt striding in.

When he saw us, he stopped. Fury snarled his face. "What's going on here?" he thundered. With long strides, he marched to Eli and knocked the ladle from his hand. Water splashed to the ground.

Mr. Pitt raised a hand as if to strike.

Eli took a step back, his eyes lowered.

"Mr. Pitt!" I exclaimed. "It's my fault. I told him to drink —"

Mr. Pitt glared at me. "It's none of your business, boy."

I stood tall and firm, my eyes locked on Mr. Pitt's. "I gave him the orders."

"No one gives orders around here except for me," Mr. Pitt said.

"We can't do good work without water and food," I told him.

"I don't pay you to be impertinent, James," Mr. Pitt said. "I pay you to do a good day's work. And I don't see much work done."

I looked up at the roof and all the patching we'd done. "Sir," I began, then stopped. I didn't want to lose my job.

Mr. Pitt's fury turned to weariness. He dropped his raised fist. "Go on home, James. I hope you've learned your lesson."

I stood looking from Mr. Pitt to Eli. I feared what might happen when I left, but I had no choice. I strode out of the barn and began the long ride home, my pockets empty of pay.

CHAPTER 7

FREEDOM AND FEAR

Eli

I got a good beating after James left. Deserved it, I s'pose. If I hadn't let Betsy the cow die, Massah Pitt wouldn't have hired the white boy. And I wouldn't be in such trouble now.

That white boy James had a lot to learn about Massah Pitt. First thing was to obey orders. I figured James had never taken orders from anyone before. And hadn't worked a day in his life. I could tell by his slow way of doing things. Massah Pitt should've hired a more able boy. But I weren't about to say nothing.

Second thing James needed to learn was not to stand up for a slave like me. That kind of action would do no good for nobody.

I woke that night to a sound in my shack. I couldn't see nothing in the dark, so I laid still. Then a soft hand nudged my cheek. It were Daisy, the house slave.

"I brought you somethin' to eat," she whispered.

"You shouldn't be here," I said. "Or you'll get a beating too."

"Massah Pitt is snorin' to the high heavens."

Massah Pitt didn't let Daisy and me talk to each other. He said we might get an idea of insurrection, which I took to mean he thought we'd run off. But Daisy never paid much mind. She chattered at me every time Massah weren't around.

I took the bundle of food. "You best be off." I said.

But Daisy didn't move. "I were in town today," she said. "Some Simpson slaves run off, I heard."

"So what?" I said. "That don't mean nothing to me. They'll be caught soon enough."

"Not if they make it to Nashville," Daisy whispered. "The Northerners run that city now. And they don't send slaves back to their masters, I hear."

"Don't be getting any ideas," I warned. "Now go on and let me eat."

After Daisy left, I thought about them Simpson slaves, out in the dark. Fearing for their lives. Just to be free. I wasn't sure freedom was worth the fear.

But as I rolled back onto my pallet, my wounds fresh and hurting, I wondered if maybe freedom really was worth the risk.

CHAPTER 8

DOUBTS

James

When I returned home, I found Mama on the sofa, staring dully at Nellie's doll, Matilda.

"I don't know why Nellie doesn't play with her anymore," Mama murmured as I entered.

"I suppose Nellie is growing too old for dolls," I told her, trying to be gentle even though I felt a pang of anger. We had so much hunger and grief, but all Mama worried about was a doll?

I didn't tell Mama or Nellie I'd returned home with no pay, and no food either.

As I lay in bed that night, I thought about Mr. Pitt. I was grateful that he'd hired me, but I'd never realized he could be so mean and heartless. I knew he wasn't a bad man at heart. My father would never have been friends with him if he were.

When I closed my eyes, I saw the red welts on Eli's shoulders that I'd pretended not to see. *What did Eli do to deserve such a beating?* I wondered. Certainly owners didn't beat their slaves for no reason.

I couldn't help but remember a time before the war when a group of abolitionists came to town. They had marched toward the town square, yelling against slavery.

Stefan and I had gathered with other onlookers to watch. One man with a loud booming voice told of the suffering of slaves at the hand of their masters. He said slaves were beaten and starved, some to death. His stories had seemed so impossible that I laughed aloud, nudging Stefan in the ribs.

Stefan didn't return my smile. He only stared, entranced, as the abolitionist continued to speak.

The crowd around me had started laughing too. Some picked up small rocks to throw at the abolitionists. Soon the group was run out of town.

"You didn't really believe all that, did you?" I asked Stefan later.

He shrugged. "I suppose some of it was true."

"You know those abolitionists just want to start trouble," I told him. "Most of them are downright crazy."

But now, after seeing Mr. Pitt's treatment of Eli, I

wondered if perhaps the abolitionists' terrible stories were indeed true.

⌐∽

The next morning I arrived at Mr. Pitt's early, while the sky was still dark as night. Most of the house's windows were dark except for the kitchen. I could see Mr. Pitt's house girl Daisy moving about the stove. Her eyes looked tired, though her movements were swift.

I couldn't help but stand and look in at Daisy. I wondered what her life was like. I wondered if she had family or friends. I wondered if she got much sleep.

I'd never stopped to think much about slaves and their lives. In the South, we all assumed slaves were happy being slaves. They had roofs over their heads and food in their bellies. Whenever I heard about slaves running off, I figured they would eventually regret it, even if they weren't caught.

Daisy seemed happy enough on the outside. But as I watched, I noticed she seemed nervous. She kept glancing behind her, eyes wide.

I went into the barn, and Eli and I set to work on patching the barn's roof. We said nothing about what had happened the day before. But as we worked, I saw a new red welt on Eli's shoulder. Guilt wrapped itself deep inside me. I knew it was my fault.

CHAPTER 9

DAISY'S IDEAS

Eli

I didn't let my wounds slow me down none. For a time, my shoulders ached when I turned a certain way. Soon, though, the welts became scars just like all the others.

That white boy James seemed to catch on to working. He were eager to please, and after that first day, he went home with money in his pocket every night.

The worst part about James was his mouth. For a few days, we worked in quiet. But then he started chattering. Told me all about his daddy, who died in the fighting in town. And all about his mama, who sulked about the house and hardly ate, even if there was food. He talked, too, about his angry little sister.

I didn't say nothing. James's problems were bad, it's sure. But I couldn't help thinkin' about my own mama, who I'd never see again. I wondered where she was and if she ever thought about me.

Whenever Mr. Pitt came around, James stopped talking. But Mr. Pitt weren't around much. He'd gotten back into gambling, I reckoned.

Once, James asked where Mr. Pitt went all the time. He said, "If he'd lend a hand, the farm would be back in shape in no time."

I shrugged. Mr. Pitt weren't a working man. Just gave orders, and that was it.

Those days, Daisy was all jittery. I'd see her lookin' out at me like she had something to say. One day, she said it. She passed me on the way to the water pump, barely pausing as she spoke. "'Member I told you about them Simpson slaves running off? One of 'em was my brother."

"They ain't been caught yet," I said.

Daisy looked proud. "And they won't!" she said. "But I aim to find 'em."

I wanted to shake her. A girl like her wouldn't make it far without getting caught. "You stay put," I told her.

I might've said more, but just then James rounded the corner. Daisy scurried off. A chill spread over me, and it weren't from the cold. I were scared for Daisy.

Then I shook off the feeling. I couldn't care. Worst thing a slave could do was care about someone. Because any moment they could be gone.

CHAPTER 10

RUINED

James

I had hoped that the money I was bringing home would raise Mama's spirits. But even on her good days, she'd only give me a half-smile and say, "Bless Mr. Pitt."

"Yes. But I worked hard for that pay," I told her.

"Of course you did," she'd say, still smiling with an empty look in her eyes.

Most days, though, Mama wasn't feeling well. We had to survive on Nellie's attempts at biscuits, grits, and wedges of overcooked meat. At Mr. Pitt's farm, I often smelled wafts of food coming from the kitchen, and I felt jealous.

One day I received a letter from Stefan. I didn't open it and almost threw it into the fire. But I stuffed it into a drawer instead.

Those days, Nellie's poor doll Matilda still sat discarded in the corner. Looking at it, I realized why

Mama had been so sad about the doll. She had seen that Nellie was too overcome by the burdens of our household to play.

I had wanted to keep Mama from discovering that I worked alongside a slave. But one night, as we sat around the table, my daddy's spot sorely bare, I made the mistake of mentioning Eli.

"Eli? Who's Eli?" Mama asked.

"Mr. Pitt's field servant," I said, hoping Mama would ask no more questions.

"A slave!" Nellie chimed in. She grinned and looked down at her plate.

I glared at her. I knew she resented Mama, but it angered me to see Nellie hurt her on purpose.

Mama set down her fork. Her eyes were wide as she looked at me. "You work with a . . . slave?" Her voice fell to a whisper as she uttered the final word.

"Yes, Mama, I do," I told her. I knew she would be upset. But I wasn't prepared for the wail that erupted from her chest.

"This dreadful war!" she cried. "We are ruined."

Mama heaved loud, wracking sobs. Nellie stared at her, half-frightened and half-remorseful.

"He's a good slave," I tried to tell Mama, but my words sounded foolish. And to Mama, it wouldn't matter if he were a good slave or a bad slave or some-where in between. The fact that he was a slave was all that mattered. And to her, my working alongside him brought our family to the lowest level of shame.

I tried once more. "I'm more of an overseer," I said. The lie brought me more shame than the truth.

But Mama didn't hear me through her crying.

Although my stomach still felt empty, I couldn't eat another bite. My family was falling apart around me, and it seemed nothing I did could help.

That night I opened Stefan's letter.

Dear James,

I know you do not wish to hear from me. And I do not know if my letter will get through. But I am lonely here at camp. It does me good to write you, even though you may never read my words.

Colonel Richardson says I won't be sent to battle, due to my age. But I drill with the regiment and have picket duty. Sometimes at night a fiddle plays, and a few fellows dance around. I never take part. I suppose I'm too serious for dancing. I am not sure how those boys can dance and laugh knowing they'll be doing some killing soon. William — a friend here — tells me I think too much. I think you have said the same thing a time or two.

Mostly I help in the medical tent, bringing in supplies and water and whatever the doctor needs. Men fall sick daily from dysentery or cough.

All we eat is hardtack, salt pork, and coffee. We sleep in tents on the hard ground. I don't sleep much. When I do, my dreams are about sleeping in a real bed again.

I've not yet seen a battle. But I am prepared.

Please write. I am lonely here.

> *Truly,*
>
> *Stefan*

I crumpled the letter and threw it back into the drawer. I would not write him. And I would feel good sleeping in my soft bed tonight.

CHAPTER 11

MAMA'S SONGS

Eli

That James never quit talkin'. Now he started tellin' me about his friend Stefan who'd joined the Yankees. Betrayed the South, he said.

To crowd out his endless talkin', I started to hum as we chopped firewood and gathered hay. A tune I'd made up from bits of my Mama's songs.

James quieted for a bit. Then broke in. "What song is that?" he asked.

"Learned it from my mama, Massah," I muttered. "Afore she were sold."

James didn't say nothin' for a while. Then he asked, "Do you miss her?"

I shrugged. "It's just the way things be for us."

He didn't say nothin' else, so I started up my tune again.

CHAPTER 12

RAIDERS

James

The days rushed by. We chopped wood, fed chickens, groomed horses, and milked cows that Mr. Pitt had won by gambling.

I kept my shotgun close as we worked. Bands of murderous raiders were sweeping across Tennessee, stealing livestock and burning buildings.

Mid-November, the wind whipped the clouds into giant gray monsters that moved across the sky. Eli and I worked until a freezing rain soaked us. The rain turned quick into sleet.

"Early season storm," Mr. Pitt said, motioning me into the house. "Best stay here overnight. Your poor old mare will never make it."

I was afraid Mama would worry herself sick when I didn't return home, but there was no way to get word to her. And oh my, the smell of Daisy's cooking tempted me to stay.

We feasted on boiled ham, bread, and corn grits, and finished our meal with blackberry tea. I thought I'd sleep good and hard after such a delicious meal, but the wind tore about the windows and kept jolting me awake.

Late in the night, I heard a noise. It wasn't the wind. Someone was downstairs.

Raiders.

I snatched my gun and stepped quietly down the stairs. I couldn't see a thing in the darkness. I paused and listened.

Silence. All I could hear was the roar of my beating heart.

Then floorboards creaked. The sound was coming from the back of the house, near the kitchen. I thought about creeping back upstairs and waking Mr. Pitt, but I knew I didn't have enough time. I had to act quickly.

I grabbed a kerosene lamp from the hall table and turned it to a low light, then took a deep breath. I would charge into the kitchen and surprise the intruder. Hopefully I wouldn't have to shoot.

I tiptoed toward the kitchen, then kicked open the door and held the blazing lantern high. "Stop right there!" I cried, dropping the lantern and raising my gun.

In the glow of light, I saw the intruder, staring at me with big eyes. My galloping heart slowed its pace.

"Daisy," I said and lowered my gun.

But Daisy's fear didn't lessen upon seeing it was me. Instead, she yelped and swiveled about on one foot, leaping toward the back door. A bundle fell from her hands and clattered to the floor. She froze.

I nudged the bundle with my foot and it fell open. A loaf of bread. And several pieces of silver.

Daisy broke into heavy, wheezing sobs. "P-p-please," she whispered.

I raised my gun and pointed it at her. Mr. Pitt's order flooded into my mind: *Shoot any slaves trying to escape.* My hands trembled.

Daisy stopped sniffling and stared at the barrel with wide, fearful eyes.

"Where are you going with that?" I demanded.

Daisy swallowed. "I were just gonna polish the silver. And take the loaf to Eli. That's all, Massah James."

I knew she was lying. She was about to either escape or help someone who had. I kept the gun level and glared at her.

"I weren't going nowhere," Daisy insisted. "I couldn't sleep and —"

"Tell your lies to Mr. Pitt," I hissed.

Daisy's head shook and then she crumpled to the floor. A low moan escaped her — the most sorrowful moan I'd ever heard.

"Get up and go to bed," I told her, "before Mr. Pitt wakes in a sour mood."

Daisy scooped herself from the floor and scrambled to put the silver back in its place.

"I'll be standing guard, so don't try anything," I warned her as she slipped from the kitchen to her quarters.

I lowered myself to a chair and rubbed my eyes. I decided I'd tell Mr. Pitt what happened first thing in the morning.

But as the night wore on, the memory of Daisy's sorrowful sob wheeled through my mind.

When morning came, I didn't say a word to Mr. Pitt.

CHAPTER 13

A KNOCK AT THE DOOR

Eli

"That white friend of yours near caught me," Daisy whispered.

I straightened and eyed her straight on. "I ain't got no white friends," I muttered, though I knew who she meant. "Catch you doin' what?"

Daisy straightened her neck and held her chin high. "Runnin' off," she said, louder than I liked.

"Don't you be tryin' that again!" I warned.

"I aim to," she said, her chin still pointing to the clouds. "You can't stop me, neither. I'm headin' out 'fore the winter comes."

"He didn't tell Massah Pitt?"

"Never had a chance to, I reckon. I was preparin' for a whipping this morning, but Massah was sweet as pie. Set off for town, and I ain't seen him since."

Just then, James rounded the corner of the barn. "Get on," I hissed to Daisy, and she scampered away.

James

That evening, I spent supper troubled by my decision. I tried talking about the awful weather to distract myself, but Mama was in a dour mood, sighing into her plate, and Nellie jiggled on her chair and pushed grits into her mouth without saying a word.

Finally I fell silent. *I should've told Mr. Pitt,* I thought. Daisy was his property. What if she tried to escape again?

Mr. Pitt had trusted me. And I'd betrayed him. What would my father have thought?

Tomorrow, I told myself. Tomorrow I would tell Mr. Pitt what Daisy had done.

A knock at the door interrupted my thoughts. Mama's knuckles whitened around her fork. "Who could that be? At this hour?"

Mr. Pitt, I thought. *He's discovered my deception and sent the jailers to arrest me.*

None of us moved. The rapping sounded again, louder this time.

Mama half-rose, but I put out a hand to stop her. "I'll answer it," I said.

I walked, knees shaking, to the door, ready to meet my punishment.

I swung open the door to find a young woman shivering on our porch. Her coat was tattered and mud-stained. Dark, wet curls flapped against her cheek. She shoved a strand of hair, in a rather unlady-like manner, from her face. Despite her pitiful appearance, she flashed me a bright, cheerful smile.

"Might I come in?" she said, in a thick accent I couldn't place. "I'm so hungry I'm nearin' certain death!"

I frowned at her. Even though I was relieved the jailers weren't after me, I felt irritated. "We've got scarce enough food to feed ourselves, let alone beggars," I said.

The girl's mouth dropped in amazement. "Are you meanin' to say you don't remember me?" she said.

Just then, Mama, who'd crept up silently behind me, shoved me aside. "Rosellen?" Mama cried. She swept the girl into a great hug.

The girl grinned at me over Mama's shoulder. "Pleasure to see you again, Jimmy. I'm your cousin Rosellen."

Mama scurried about, gathering dry clothes and a plate of food for Rosellen. I hadn't seen Mama so energized since my father died. I worried she'd overdo herself, but her cheeks were the brightest pink I'd seen in months.

As she was rushing about, she kept pausing to gaze at Rosellen. "My sister's daughter," she murmured. "You resemble her so!"

Nellie, meanwhile, never broke her stare. She sat chewing her nails and looking Rosellen up and down, as though she were a creature from another land.

"I'm sorry to drop in on you like this," Rosellen said, after she'd mouthed down two platefuls. "But I had no one else to turn to."

We were gathered around the fireplace, and Rosellen kept rubbing her hands together and holding them toward the flames. I noticed the tips of her fingers still seemed white with frost.

"Where is your family? What of your father and brothers?" Mama asked. "We lost touch after your mama died. And then . . ."

Rosellen gave a sad smile and sighed. "It's not a happy tale, but I shall tell it with pride," she said. "If you have the time, that is."

We nodded and settled in to hear Rosellen's story.

CHAPTER 14

YANKEE BETRAYAL

James

"My story begins a year ago, in November 1861," Rosellen told us. "But first I must say that my father, like many in eastern Tennessee, is a Unionist." In that part of the state, she explained, no one had big cotton plantations and few owned slaves. They didn't want to send soldiers to die just so rich Southerners could keep their slaves.

When the war began, two of her brothers joined the Union Army. Some Confederate neighbors, once their friends, now became their enemies. They ransacked and burned Unionist farms.

"Every night, I went to bed in fear," Rosellen said. "Would the Confederates burn our house down? Would my father be arrested for his views?"

"I know what it's like to have your friends turn against you," I said, thinking of Stefan.

Rosellen looked at me in surprise, but she didn't ask any questions.

"One night," she continued, "I heard my father creep out of the house. I shoved my hair in a hat and put on trousers so I looked like a boy. Then I followed him."

When her father realized Rosellen was following him, he told her to go home. But she refused.

"Growing up with all brothers taught me to stand my ground no matter what," Rosellen said. She smiled at Nellie, but Nellie only glared back.

Rosellen and her father went to a house in Elizabethton, where other Unionists had gathered. Still pretending to be a boy, Rosellen stayed at the edge of the group and kept her eyes down.

At first, the Unionists just talked about railroads. The East Tennessee & Virginia Railroad was important to the Confederates. The Confederates used it to send soldiers, supplies, and weapons to Virginia.

Rosellen was growing bored with the talk. But then she learned of the dangerous and daring plan. To stop the flow of Confederate supplies, the Unionist group would burn the railroad bridges.

My blood chilled. Here was a traitor to our cause, right in our very own home!

"You didn't, did you?" Mama whispered in disbelief.

Rosellen wouldn't meet Mama's eyes. "At first, my father didn't want me taking part. But I've never been a gentle Southern girl. I can ride faster than any boy and shoot better than any soldier. So he finally said yes."

On the night of November 8, several groups set out for nine different bridges, armed with turpentine, torches, and matches. Rosellen's group headed for the Holston River bridge. At first, it appeared unguarded. Then, two Confederate guards popped up, one on each end of the bridge.

"We sure surprised 'em," Rosellen chuckled. "One took off a runnin'. The other surrendered. When he swore to secrecy, we let him go."

The group tossed turpentine on the bridge and set it alight. Flames whooshed and crackled. The bridge splintered and crashed into the water below.

"I've never been so proud of anything in my life!" Rosellen said. "But we soon found out the others hadn't been so successful. Only five bridges were burned."

The Confederates were furious. In the days that followed, they rounded up anyone suspected to be part of the plot. That winter, they hanged two of the bridge-burners.

"I couldn't stop thinking about the rebel guard we'd

set free," Rosellen told us. She shivered. "What if he talked?"

And sure enough, one day the Confederates came and took her father away. Rosellen, fearing her part in the plot would be discovered, fled to Elizabethton to stay with friends. Her father was still in prison, awaiting trial.

"No one would suspect me, a girl, for taking part," Rosellen said. "But even so, my Unionist friends risked their lives by harboring me. I couldn't put them in danger anymore, so I came here. I'm at your mercy, now."

CHAPTER 15

TRUTH OR LIES

James

After Rosellen finished her story, I leapt to my feet. Anger flared in my heart as quickly as if Rosellen had lit it with a match and turpentine. "Traitor!" I cried. "We'll not harbor you, either. You'd best be on your way, or I'll alert the Confederate Home Guard."

Rosellen didn't seem surprised. She nodded. "Yes, I'm a traitor. I admit it. But I beg you to allow me to stay. As punishment for my actions, I will devote my time to the Confederate cause."

I sat speechless. Finally I managed, "First you're a traitor, and now you're a turncoat?"

Mama didn't give Rosellen a chance to reply. "I've always believed in justice," she said. "You are family. And you will stay."

I stared hard at Rosellen. Was she telling the truth or lies? She stared back at me, unflinching.

I couldn't make heads nor tails of it. Exhaustion

pummeled me quick as a bullet, and I marched upstairs to my room without another word. I fell fast asleep, having forgotten entirely about Daisy.

Eli

If Daisy run off, I knew Massah Pitt would have my hide. I lurked about the yard as much as I could, one eye on the house, the other on James. I couldn't figure why he never told on Daisy. Waitin' for the right moment, I figured. Could be no other reason.

For days after, James weren't his usual talking self. Seemed angry as spit, tromping about the farm like he'd rather be anywhere but here.

A few times I saw Daisy lingering at the back door. When she saw me, she ducked back inside. Where would she go after she run off? These parts were covered with Confederate soldiers and slave catchers.

Whenever Massah Pitt were around, I thought for sure James would tell him 'bout Daisy. But James barely glanced at Massah.

Once James caught me eyeing him. "What you lookin' at?" he snarled.

"Nothin', Massah James," I said.

I couldn't figure him out. He were the strangest white boy I'd ever come across.

CHAPTER 16

THE DOLL

James

I couldn't help but admire Rosellen. Even though her bridge-burning was rotten and traitorous, it was a brave thing for a girl to do. But I was suspicious of her sudden devotion to the Confederate cause. I figured she was just trying to get in good standing with the Confederates so they'd let her father go. Either that, or she was a spy.

I must admit, though, her coming was a godsend. Mama snapped out of her misery, even laughing once in a while. Mama, Nellie, and Rosellen spent their days at the church, rolling bandages and sewing shirts for our soldiers.

Rosellen took over the cooking, and the scents that wafted from the kitchen smelled like heaven itself.

Despite Rosellen's good cooking and Mama's better mood, Nellie was still angry. Now though, her anger was directed at Rosellen rather than Mama.

She started doing mean things. She poured salt into Rosellen's sweetcakes and sugar into Rosellen's meat stew. When Mama scolded her, Nellie only laughed.

Finally, one day I came home to find Rosellen and Nellie in the front room. Rosellen had Nellie's doll Matilda on her lap.

"She's so lovely. Why don't you play with her anymore?" Rosellen asked.

"I'm too old," Nellie muttered.

"She has beautiful hair! Did you braid it yourself?"

Nellie only scowled.

"All I had were brothers and no mama. I never learned but a simple braid. Will you teach me?" Rosellen said.

Nellie snatched the doll from Rosellen's lap. "It ain't hard," she said. She unraveled Matilda's hair. In minutes, she'd twisted Matilda's hair into loops and braids.

"Will you braid my hair like that?" Rosellen asked.

Nellie sighed, but I could see she wanted to. Finally she walked behind Rosellen's chair, brushed out her hair, and began braiding. She yanked harder than she should've, but Rosellen never complained.

After that, Nellie seemed to soften toward Rosellen. I'd find the two of them together by the fire, braiding Matilda's hair.

Sometimes, sitting by the fireplace with my belly full, I could pretend there was no war.

Until I received another letter from Stefan.

Dear James,

I write this letter with regret. I have witnessed my first battle. I wish I could wash my eyes of the memory and clean my ears of the sounds. I will not describe it to you other than to say the horror of battle will follow me forever.

The battle was a Union victory. But victory is a strong and joyous word. I felt no joy at all as I helped carry the wounded from the field.

I could not bear to look at the faces of the Confederate dead. What if they were my neighbors or my friends? What if I have I joined the wrong side?

But these Union boys are my friends, too.

It seems all sides are wrong.

This is why I write with regret.

I want to come home.

Truly,
Stefan

I folded the letter. I couldn't feel anger at Stefan anymore. He was suffering, too.

I didn't speak much to Rosellen. Despite the light she'd brought into our home, I didn't much trust her.

My distrust deepened one night when Rosellen stopped me in the upstairs hall. "Tell me about Eli," she said.

I stiffened. "What about him? There ain't nothing to tell. He's a slave."

"Tell me this, then," Rosellen said. "Do you think slavery is right? People should own other people, just because of skin color?"

"It's just the way things are," I told her, then looked away. I hoped she didn't see the doubt in my eyes.

"So you think Eli deserves to be a slave?" Rosellen demanded. "You think he's stupid?"

"Eli ain't stupid!" I yelled without thinking.

A smile bloomed on Rosellen's face. "If you change your mind about slavery," she said, "send Eli to me."

I stared at her, confused.

Rosellen placed a hand on my shoulder and squeezed. "Tell him I know the way," she whispered.

CHAPTER 17

CHRISTMAS GIFT

James

I wasn't about to relay Rosellen's message to Eli. And as it turned out, I would never have the chance.

The next morning, I rode to Pitt's farm. Mr. Pitt was standing on the porch, waiting for me. His eyes were rimmed red, and gray circles swooped under them.

"You've done a good job, James," Mr. Pitt said. "The farm is ready for winter now. And I'm at the last of my money."

He didn't come outright and say it, but I knew I was no longer needed. I bade Mr. Pitt farewell, then hurried to the barn to find Eli.

"You're to carry on yourself, now," I told him.

He nodded.

Without hesitation, I held out my hand for him to shake. But he only stared at my outstretched hand with confusion. I dropped my arm, gave him a quick nod, and rushed out.

As I rode home, I felt a mixture of relief, worry, and sadness. I no longer had to feel guilt about Daisy. But how would we find enough money for food? The money for my father's service still hadn't come.

And, although I could scarcely admit it even to myself, I would miss Eli.

December brought cold, Confederates, and a wedding to Murfreesboro. On December 14, one of our local girls, Martha Ready, married Confederate General John Hunt Morgan. Mama dressed in her finest, and Rosellen, Nellie, and I escorted her to the grand ball held at the courthouse.

Bands played. The chandelier glistened light upon us. Rosellen, her hair done up in curls and braids, waltzed with Confederate soldiers, one after the other. Mama, dressed in widow's black, declined to dance but accepted sympathies from General Morgan himself.

Music spilled over the town into the wee hours of the morning. The event was a bright spot in the dark days of war.

All that month, more and more Confederate soldiers poured into Murfreesboro. We knew what it meant. The Yankees were soon coming to take back the town.

Eli

Without James, work were lonely. I guess I could say I missed him.

Confederate soldiers in gray swarmed the countryside. Far as I could tell, they were readying for a battle with the blue coats.

Them gray-coated soldiers cursed and laughed and spit at me whenever I passed 'em on the roads. But in some ways, they put my mind at ease. We didn't have to worry no longer about raiders. No one would try to raid us with the Confederate soldiers so close.

All along Stones River and the road to Nashville, the soldiers forced our neighbors to leave their homes. Then they burned and tore down barns and other buildings to make room for battle.

With all them soldiers about, I figured Daisy wouldn't try to take off.

I were wrong.

Christmas morning, Massah Pitt thundered into the barn, hollerin', "Where is she?"

Dread hardened in my belly. I scurried down the ladder to face Massah Pitt.

"You knew about this," he hissed.

I couldn't lie, so I said nothin'.

We went out scourin' every corner of the fields. Daisy weren't nowhere. When we went a piece up the road, soldiers stopped us. Massah Pitt said we was huntin' a runaway. But the soldiers made us turn back.

I knew what were coming to me. And I were right. That night I got a hard beating.

A fine Christmas gift.

CHAPTER 18

YANKEE VISITORS

James

A few days after the Morgan wedding, Confederate officers knocked on our door. Before I had a chance to open it, they barged in.

Nellie huddled in the corner while the officers stomped about our house, soiling our rugs with their muddy boots. They ordered us to clear our belongings out of our rooms, and then they settled in.

Mama, Nellie, and Rosellen shared a tiny room off the kitchen, and I made myself a bed on the back porch.

The soldiers tromped in and out at all hours. Every night, we served them dinner from our meager pantry. I worried they would discover Rosellen's Unionist ways, but she charmed them with her smile and her devotion to the Southern cause. She often winked at me, as though we shared a secret.

Whenever I could, I listened to the officers' talk. The Union soldiers were on the march from Nashville. Word was, soldiers in blue stretched along the Nashville road, far as the eye could see. Confederate General Bragg lined our boys along the Stones River, ready to stop them in their tracks.

I knew every nook and cranny of Stones River. I could picture our boys in gray, camped in the places Stefan and I had made our forts and fought pretend battles. This time, the battle would be real.

I wondered where Stefan was now.

We in Murfreesboro knew the battle would be a big one, and we prayed for a Confederate victory. The thought of Federals crawling about the town again made my stomach churn.

With any battle comes wounded. I helped clear schools and churches of furniture for makeshift hospitals. And then we waited.

Eli

The thunder of hooves woke me right up. *Soldiers,* I thought. *Comin' to take over Pitt's farm. But why in the middle of the night?*

I nudged open the door of my shack. The moon was round and shone white light over the farmyard.

Near a dozen soldiers on horseback circled the house. I stepped closer, about to holler at 'em.

Then I saw. Them soldiers weren't in gray.

They wore blue.

Yankees.

I had to warn Massah Pitt. Quiet as I could, I crept toward the back door. But two soldiers stood guard, guns gleamin' in the moonlight.

I stayed hidden in the shadows and made my way to the front of the house.

"Come on out here!" a soldier called toward the house.

I watched the windows. Nothin'. Where were Massah Pitt?

The soldier turned to his men. "Burn it down," he ordered.

Just then, the front door swung open. Massah Pitt appeared, wearin' his nightclothes. "I ain't leavin'!" he cried. And with that, he raised his gun.

Shots rang out. Massah Pitt fell and tumbled down the porch steps.

The soldiers jumped over Massah's body and ran into the house, comin' back out with armloads of silver and dishes. Then they set the house alight. Flames crackled, reachin' up toward the moon.

Meantime, other soldiers kicked open the barn door and shoved our cows, mooing frightened-like, into the yard. They knocked down fences and gathered chickens into their sacks.

Flames whooshed through the barn, lighting up the night sky.

Everythin' happened in seconds. I couldn't do nothin' to stop 'em. I had no gun. So I crouched in the trees, watchin' the only home I knew burn to the ground.

Them soldiers were gone as fast as they'd come. Their laughter scorched the air as they went gallopin' down the lane, our horses and cows in tow.

I rushed to Massah Pitt, fearin' the worst. He were shot in the shoulder, just near the heart, but he were still breathin'. He opened his eyes as I bent over him.

I ripped off my shirt and wrapped it around his wound.

"Don't you worry, Massah Pitt," I told him. "I'm gonna get help!"

I didn't know what to do. All our neighbors had fled. Who could I turn to?

Then I knew. Without another thought, I broke into a run. Headin' toward Murfreesboro.

CHAPTER 19

HOME SWEET HOME

Eli

I picked my way through the woods. Runnin' when I could, hidin' when I had to. I didn't trust no one, now. Not the Confederates. Not the Federals. Seemed everyone was my enemy.

I crawled along a ridge above Stones River. Scattered campfires glowed. I could see soldiers moving from tent to tent. Far off, more fires burned. I knew it were the Union soldiers.

Then I heard a curious sound. Music.

The song "Home Sweet Home" rose into the air. Strange enough, it seemed to come from both sides.

Home. I had no home now.

But the truth was, Pitt's farm hadn't felt like home since Mama left. I had nothing to lose by leaving, that was for sure.

Wherever Mama was, that was home.

Crouchin' low, I scampered down the ridge toward Murfreesboro. I didn't have much time. And Massah Pitt, he didn't neither.

CHAPTER 20

UNDERGROUND RAILROAD

James

I slept fitfully on the porch. And it wasn't just the cold. Every small sound woke me. And when I did sleep, I dreamed I was on the banks of Stones River, surrounded by Federals. They shot at me and I ran. I was looking for something, someone. Stefan.

Near dawn, I woke to scratching on the screen door. A wind had come up, and I figured it was just a dead branch blowing by. I rolled over to go back to sleep.

But then I heard the sound again. A twig snapped, and a shadow moved against the window.

Someone was here.

I stiffened.

Then I heard a familiar voice calling softly. "Massah James?"

I peered out and saw Eli staring up at the upstairs

windows. He was about to call again when I hissed, "Eli!"

He nearly jumped out of his skin.

I swung open the door and waved to him.

"Massah James!" he said. "What you doin' on the porch?"

"What are you doing here?" I answered.

Eli clambered up the steps, breathless.

"It's Massah Pitt," he said in a rush. "He been shot. Men in blue came, torched the place, left Massah for dead. I dunno if they were soldiers or just pretendin' to be. We gotta help him!"

I stared at him, shocked.

I didn't know what to do. All the doctors in town were out at the army camp. By the time I found someone, it might be too late.

I felt around for my boots and coat. "We'll saddle up the horse," I said, "and bring him back to town."

Eli nodded. Then his eyes widened, and he stared at something over my shoulder.

"Not so fast," a voice said.

Eli

One of the prettiest girls I ever saw stepped out onto the porch. And she had a gun in her hand.

I about fell off the steps in haste to get away. "Stop!" she said, and I froze.

I glanced up at her, and she were smiling. "I'm Rosellen. And I'm about to set you free."

"Free, miss?" I choked.

She kept smiling. "I heard everything," she said. "And now is your time! Mr. Pitt's farm is long gone. He'll have no need for you. He'll just sell you off. You don't want that, do you?"

I frowned. "I dunno, miss," I said.

She motioned for me to come closer. Then she told us about somethin' called the Underground Railroad. The railroad led slaves to freedom. It weren't really underground, just a secret. And it weren't a railroad at all, just homes along the way where slaves could hide.

As she talked, I kept starin' at the gun in her hand. Finally she held it out to me. "This is for you," she said. "For protection."

I wasn't sure I wanted to go. But freedom were close. So close.

And maybe, once I were free, I could find Mama.

"Take the east road," Rosellen said. "You'll see a house with a lantern on the hitching post. That's a sign of a safe house. Hurry, before dawn breaks."

"But Massah Pitt —" I began.

James ain't said a word the whole time. Now he spoke up. "Go!" he said. "We'll take care of Mr. Pitt."

I took Rosellen's gun and made to leave off.

"Wait!" James called. He held out his hand. "Farewell, Eli."

I ain't never shook a white boy's hand before. But this time I did. "Farewell, Massah James," I said.